The Little Bear
And
The Big Bear

The Little Bear and The Big Bear

Written and Illustrated by Monica Dumont

To my pebbles, Dhara.

With love from auntie.

And to all the other beautiful children in my life.

Once there was a big angry bear and a
little happy bear

that lived in the deep, deep forest.

The big angry bear was always growling
and stomping, doing whatever it is big
bears do during the day.

GRRR...

GRRR...

GRRR...

STOMP!

STOMP!

STOMP!

STOMP!

The little bear was always just happy
while doing whatever it is little bears do.

One day the little bear went to
play by the creek.
He noticed that the big bear was
there too,

but instead of playing he was just
growling and stomping.

The little bear decided to take a closer look at what was happening and saw the big bear all tangled up in his skipping rope.

He then noticed that the more the
big bear growled and stomped, the
more tangled he got.

He went closer to the big bear and asked if
he could help,

but the big bear felt that maybe no one could help because things were always so difficult.

The little bear looked him straight in the eye and said, "Things are what they are, but they are always changing."

"What I do," the little bear said, "is whenever I feel frustrated, I stop."

"I go do something else. Then I come back and start all over again, taking it one step at a time"

The big bear smiled for the first time in
a long, long time.

And together they learned a new way of skipping rope.

The End

Book Challenge:

Like big bear, you can also improve the way you deal with situations by changing the way you see them.

Step 1: Ask one of your parents, a guardian or an adult you like, to help you think of three situations or events in your personal life that felt bad when they happened. Then discuss how they started to become better as time passed.

Step 2: Now think of a situation you would like to improve in your personal life.

Step 3: Talk to your adult friend about how your particular situation in step 2 will improve in the future. Then discuss how you can start improving things in this situation **one small step at a time.**

Step 4: Use the step by step chart to help you check off each step as you accomplish them.

Please note:
This exercise is meant to help parents bond with their child as well as to help their child develop new skills at dealing with everyday life. It is not meant to be used as a form of therapy.

My Step by Step Chart 1

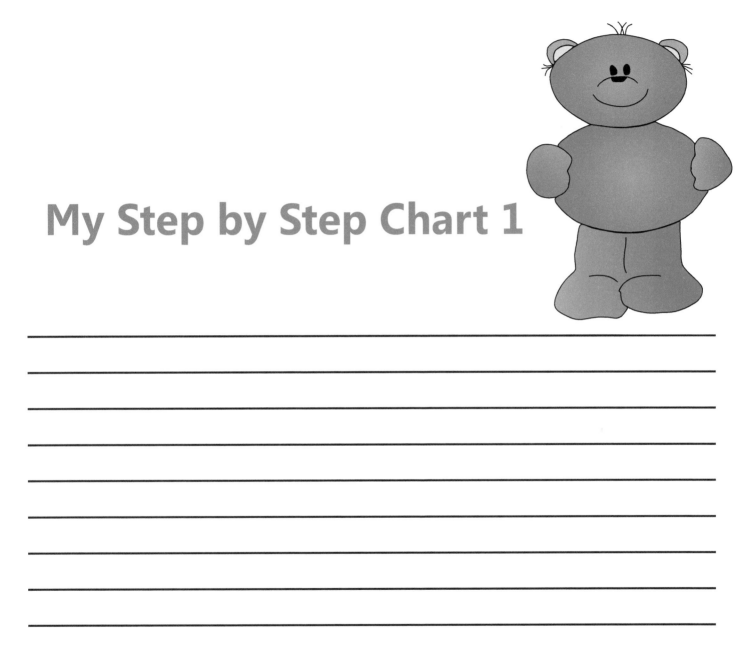

_____

_____

_____

_____

_____

_____

_____

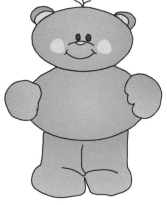

My Step by Step Chart 2

_____

_____

_____

_____

_____

_____

_____

_____

_____

_____

My Step by Step Chart 3

_____

_____

_____

_____

_____

_____

_____

_____

_____

_____

_____

Colour us

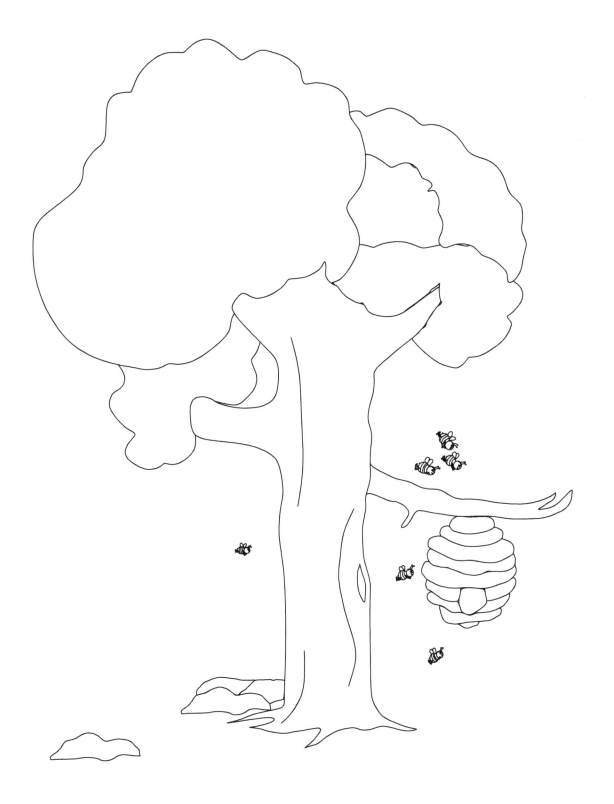

CPSIA information can be obtained
at www.ICGtesting.com
Printed in the USA
LVHW070731250720
661486LV00030B/2654